THE SAME WIND

BY BETTE KILLION

ILLUSTRATIONS BY BARBARA BUSTETTER FALK

A Laura Geringer Book
An Imprint of HarperCollinsPublishers

Library of Congress Cataloging-in-Publication Data
Killion, Bette.
    The same wind / by Bette Killion ; illustrations by Barbara
Bustetter Falk.
       p.   cm.
    "A Laura Geringer book."
    Summary: A girl asks if the wind that blows through her curtains
at night is the same wind to be found playing with tumbleweeds,
building a tornado, or teasing a sail on a tropical river.
    ISBN 0-06-021050-8.—ISBN 0-06-021051-6 (lib. bdg.)
    [1. Winds—Fiction.]   I. Falk, Barbara Bustetter, ill.
II. Title.
PZ7.K5576Sam   1992   92-7786
[E]—dc20   CIP
                                                 AC

To Beth, who once asked
—Bette Killion

To Juliana
—Barbara Bustetter Falk

Wind in the night sky
that hurries the ragged clouds
along a moon path.

Are you the same wind
that shakes the leafy summer trees
and rocks the owlets to sleep
in their nests?

Wind

that sweeps over the forests
of the North and stalks the
black bear in his den.

Are you the same wind
that brushes the arms of the tall saguaro cactus
and plays games with the tumbleweed?

Wind
that drives a summer storm over the pastures
where sheep huddle together, watching
the lightning streak the skies
while thunder crashes.

Are you the same wind
that gathers dark clouds
over the lone stray dog
who roams the countryside
looking for friends and a home?

Wind
that runs up the mountains,
whistles over the rocky slopes and ledges,
and listens to the old, old stories
that the ancient bristlecone pines tell.

Are you the same wind
that cries over the southern swamps,
moving the dark, murky waters where
the cypress trees wade to their knees,
and the alligators sleep,
slapping their tails?

Wind
that blows over the warm tropical river,
teasing a flapping sail.
Are you rippling the waters
to find the manatee,
who lies lazily feeding
in the shallow quiet below you?

Or are you a faraway Netherlands wind
that drives the long arms of the windmills,
rustles the fields of tulips,
and taunts the long-legged, clattering storks
where they nest on the rooftops?

Are you the same wind
that flutters the leaves in the vegetable garden
and drives away the pilfering pig?

Wind
that patterns the soft rain
over the spring meadow,
where the long grasses hide
new wildflowers
and a shy, creeping box turtle.

Are you the same wind
—the angry wind—
that builds a dark, swirling tornado
over the rolling flatlands,
charging and roaring and smashing
everything in your path
until even the prairie dog hides
in his burrow?

Wind,
if you are the same wind,
why do you blow so gently in my window?